BRII OF KINGS

An Oaths of Blood Saga Novella

Logan D. Irons

LOGANIRONS.COM

Copyright © 2023 by Logan D. Irons

All rights reserved.

No portion of this book may be reproduced in any form without written permission from the publisher or author, except as permitted by U.S. copyright law.

Contents

Epigraph	IV
I	1
II	16
III	28
IV	38
V	42
VI	57
A Word From Logan	64
About the Author	66

*"Where wolf's ears are, wolf's teeth are near." -
Volsunga Saga*

I

Northern England, 1066

To the south, carrion birds were an angry smoke swirling in the sky. The black cloud spread out above a distant hill, an aerial embodiment of the bitter violence that scarred the land beneath them. A saying his mother had always told him resonated in the recess of his mind: *Only death resides below a crow's dark wings.*

Ulf Bodvarsson leaned on the steering oar of his longship, the handle smooth from years in his palm, the salt from the water ground deep in the grain. His strength and weight easily guided the shallow-bottom vessel around a fallen tree bending in the river's current. He eyed the cloud of scavenging birds again. Odin's wolves had descended unto the English kingdom leaving the corpses of the defiant in their bloody wake, the scavengers of land fat of belly and crimson of beak.

His men had caught eye of the birds now. They kept silent and worked the oars, each oar blade cutting the water in unison. The crew bent hard on their benches, muscles in their backs, shoulders, and legs straining with practiced flexion. His warriors were as at home with an oar in hand as they were with sword and axe. For to his men, the sea and battlefield were, above all else, the best parts of life.

The people of these lands called this river Drewent, and its current was strong, strong enough to sweep a man far downriver before he gained his composure if he was an adept swimmer. If he was a poor swimmer, Ran's net could ignominiously steal his life, forcing him to join her in Aegir's hall. While the crew's eyes drifted toward the sky, the soft thump of Floki's drum kept them rowing in time. But all knew that a massive battle had been fought with many dead to attract such a horde of the eaters of dead.

"Odin's birds feast on our brothers' victory," said Erik over his shoulder as he rowed. His beard and hair were braided in single braids, blazing strands of a setting orange sun.

"Pray to Odin that we haven't missed the entire war," said Halfdan, his voice deep and broken from a massive scar running along the side of his neck where a Scoti spear had almost sent him to the afterlife. His hair reminded Ulf of wheat after harvest. "To row all this way for nothing would be a cruel jest by the gods."

"It is hotter than Eitri's forge here. Does this land never cool?" asked Knud. He had a plain wide face with clever eyes, his favored weapon a spear with a duo of throwing axes. He could throw them interchangeably in either hand with deadly accuracy. The crew around him grumbled their agreement. It was far too late in the year for such warm weather.

"We will see the enemy before long," called Ulf. Crow's-feet ran from the corners of piercing blue eyes, the rims encircled with gold beneath a domineering brow. A trimmed but long gray and brown beard pointed from his chin in a long braid to the center of his chest. A wolf's head made of gold dangled from the braid's tip. His hair was long and gray, arrow shafts of brown streaked through it clinging stubbornly to existence.

A bronze scale cuirass hung down to his thighs, a mail coat underneath draped to his elbows.

His men's eagerness in the face of battle stirred pride in his chest. They were known as the Lochlainn, those who came from the land of lakes. Fierce warriors who inhabited the harsh rocky islands to the far north of the Kingdom of Alba. Men as lean and harsh as the islands they raided from. The same northern islands that were the steppingstones for King Harald Hardrada's massive invasion of England to claim a crown promised to him long ago by a dead king with no heirs. A king who had promised his kingdom to anyone within earshot.

A wooden bridge came into his view. It spanned the river in the distance, leaving two gaps beneath that his longship, without its mast erect, could carefully navigate. He tasted the winds and found the potent mixture of many men and fires. He'd expected the encampment; it was the one they sought to join. This scent overcame the softer redolence of the land that was both a foreign yet familiar blend of grass, timber, rocks, and water.

"Floki, we near the camp," he called to the drummer. The grizzled warrior was a bulky man with a shaven head and a lean in his back from a fall off a cliff that left him slow in gait and weak on a sea bench. The rhythm decreased on the drum, and the warriors on the benches followed his lead, slowing their pace.

Soon a sprawling encampment sprung to life roughly a thousand paces away from the river's embankment and on a slight crest of a hill. Ulf could make out the clusters of hide tents and fires, tendrils of smoke trickling skyward. The Norse warriors moved among the tents. He noted the lack of protective fortifications around the camp, no sharpened stakes or ditches to impede an enemy assault.

He leaned into the rudder, letting his weight gradually guide the longship toward shore. He aimed for a group of six of longships beached near the wooden bridge. "Styrbord," he barked at his men.

The longships rested on their sides upon the river's embankment far enough out of the water to not be pulled back adrift by the current. His men struggled to row the final stretch, but experience and strength prevailed over the rushing waters, and Ulf guided the *Sea Raven* upon the muddy shore. The embankment begrudgingly embraced them as they forced the ship upon her. Grass billowed from the tops of the river's edge, moving with a soft breeze.

"Keep your armor and arms with you," Ulf called to his men. Oars were turned upward then stored inside the ship. They secured weapons on belts, and donned mail and leather armor before checking that their sea chests were secure.

Knud leapt into the shallows, rope in hand. "Even the waters are warm," he said with a laugh.

"That's because it's English piss," Erik said.

Knud laughed over his shoulder. "They heard old Floki was coming to feed them his fish stew and they pissed themselves."

Floki frowned at the young men. "I don't see why you're complaining. It is a recipe of your mother's."

"Do not speak of her in ill, old man," Knud called back, slogging onto the embankment.

Erik grinned beneath his fiery beard. "No wonder Knud's so small. A boy could never grow into a man eating such wretched fare."

"She wasn't known for her cooking," Floki said with a mischievous grin then he called to Knud. "You might be one of mine, boy."

Knud spit in his direction and climbed the riverbank, searching for a place to secure the longship.

A faint scent lingering in the air caught Ulf's nose, making it twitch. It was a foreign mixture, fear and hate. He scanned the woodline on the opposing side of the river but couldn't discern any cause. Two crews of Norse congregated near the opposite side of the bridge. The men watched on as two men partook in *glima*, wrestling one another until one could disengage with advantage. Shields leaned against upturned spears and swords stuck in the ground. Horns were raised to lips as the men cheered on the opponents. He dismissed the scent as a heated match between the men.

He unhooked his shield from a nearby peg, a black wolf's head painted over a field of white and secured his helm on his belt. Finally, he collected his long axe known as Crowfeeder and leapt from the prow of his longship, splashing in the shallow water.

His bronze scale and ring-mail armor clinked softly as he landed. More of his men followed and ropes were tossed down. His men separated into two groups, and they dragged the ship farther onto the riverside before fastening the ropes to a large tree.

"Current is strong," Erik said, peering at the waters nearby.

"Aye, it will be with us when we leave this place."

"But not soon. We have lands to plunder."

Ulf's lip curled in amusement. "Gods willing, you will return home a rich man."

"With wetted blade."

"I am sure we will get to kill something before we depart."

Erik shaded his eyes from the harshness of the sun, watching the men grappling for advantage. "I would test myself against them," he said with a longing glance. "I have only lost thrice since I've come of age."

Ulf considered the young warrior, a sense of pride rising in him. "You have much of your father in you. He always found a fight. No matter the man's size, he never backed down. Every day, you share more of his look."

Erik grinned and rolled his neck. "My grandfather always said we were blessed with giant's fire in the veins."

"Of that I have no doubt."

Erik's grandfather carried the same trait as did his father before him, both men known to Ulf. Now he stood sentinel over the family's kin as he would his own. With the passing of each generation, he became more callous than the last. To watch the things you love grow and die was a bitter part of his existence that most men could never understand. "Keep your wits about you. These lands are not friendly to us."

A wide grin split the red-bearded man's face, and he gathered Halfdan and Knud before crossing the bridge to test their mettle against the other warriors. Forearms were gripped and the warriors disappeared into the crowd of spectators.

"Hail, brother," came a shout from a distance. Ulf turned. Two men on horseback traveled from the immense encampment in his direction. A smile forced its way onto Ulf's lips as he recognized a friend he had not seen in years. He lifted his axe in the air in a greeting of warriors. "Hail, brother."

With long strides, Ulf met them halfway. Gray hair had taken root in his friend's beard as though he had walked through a blizzard, the flakes congregating along his ears before fading across his jaw, the beard wrapping above his lips, leaving his chin bare. The two men stared at one another.

"Hardrada," he said.

"You are late, Ulf Bodvarsson."

"Is the war over?"

"Not until I drink from that upstart cur's bloody skull."

"Then I have arrived just in time." Ulf eyed his friend from years long past. Hardrada was a massive man, even larger than Ulf himself, his horse appearing almost a pony beneath him. Where Ulf was the wolf, Hardrada was the bear. He wore a fine blue tunic, heavy gold chain dangling around his neck, and belted upon his hip was an elegant sword longer than most, the sheath inlaid with gold. "It is just like you to rush into a fight before I arrive."

"I've never been a patient man."

"No, Hardrada, you aren't."

"That is *King* Harald Sigurdsson," said the man next to Hardrada. Like the king, he was unarmored. His stature was formidable, one of apparent noble upbringing, but he was smaller and far leaner than the king. His cheeks held a gaunt, almost hollow, appearance as if he had missed meals on purpose, and a long golden mustache dominated his face. His tunic was a finely embroidered green with gold.

Ulf addressed the unknown man curtly, "I know him as the Hardrada."

"They say it is for my hard rule," Hardrada said, the truth hidden in his smirk.

"When I knew you, it came for another reason."

Hardrada barked a laugh. "I am glad to see you again. To think you answered my call to war. The gods have smiled upon me."

"I would not neglect a brother in need," Ulf said. His eyes drifted to the king's encamped army. "However, you must have over two hundred ships here. Tell me of what has transpired in my absence."

The king's companion spoke. "God has granted us a great victory over the usurper lords Morcar and Edwin." He cocked his head to the side. "My lands will soon be restored to me, God willing."

"The gods have been on our side," Hardrada said. His horse stomped a hoof punctuating the statement.

"You mean God. You have been baptized a Christian," the companion said.

"At least thrice," Hardrada said with a wink for Ulf. "I believe you were there for the first time."

"I was, and the last I saw you, you were carrying a chest with enough gold and riches to buy a kingdom. Surprised your ship did not sink."

Hardrada belted a hearty laugh. "I had a bigger ship built. *The Serpent*. You probably passed her near that dungheap Riccall."

"We did while sailing upriver. It is unwise to camp so far from the ships, but you must know this."

Hardrada grinned. "What do I have to fear from these Saxon dogs? They are routed, and now I await their gift of hostages. If they do not comply, we will raze Jórvik to the ground." His word's made his companion blanch, but he held his tongue.

"Foreign lands are never friendly for long. Few of your men wear armor. Surely all the Saxons are not defeated?"

Hardrada glanced toward the blazing sun raining heat upon them. "Those are easy words from a man who wears mail like another wears a tunic." He eyed Ulf. "The sun bears down upon us without constraint. I would not force my men to armor after the battle they fought so hard to win and the enemy running with tail between their legs."

"Donning armor in enemy lands is one of the first things you learn from the Guard."

Hardrada pointed a finger at him. "And we are no longer in the deserts and hills of the Arabs or the mountains of the Bulgars or the slopes of Etna. Saxons would probably try to hump a horse before they figured out how to ride it." A wide grin split his face, and he slapped Ulf's shoulder. "You always had a keen eye for such things. My son-in-law will be eager to join us once more. That is unless he's marched south to fight Harold himself." Hardrada laughed at the thought.

"He's a good lad?"

"Stout of heart. Strong on oar. A storm with a sword." The king raised his eyebrows. "When we return to Orkney, Orri and Maria are to be wed."

"He sounds like a fine match for Maria."

"If the union produces a boy, we can celebrate." The king's eyes narrowed. "You haven't aged a day since we last seen one another. What? Twenty years ago? When I had more seed and more fields to plow than I ever dreamed of." The aging king's eyes distanced in the foggy mists of a memory. "You know, I still dream of those days in the Guard. Life was as simple as it was easy. Crush the emperor's enemies. Make love to all the women of the East. Drink until you pass out. Wake up. Do it all again. We were in the emperor's version of Valhalla. I am surprised you ever left. Gods be good, I am surprised anyone ever leaves."

"My time there was done." He paused in reflection. "It had been too long since I visited the isles."

Hardrada spread his arms wide. "You missed those wet cold rocks in the north you call home?"

"I did. It is my home."

"Your island holds a critical port for my control of these lands. But surely no man would miss these lands filled with rebellious backstabbing lords, murderous Scots, and Saxon dogs." He glanced at his comrade. "I meant no offense, Tostig."

"None of us can help to which people we are born. We call ourselves English now." He dipped his head to the king.

"English?" Hardrada spat. "These lands are more Dane than Saxon or Angle or whatever tribe you belong too. It is my duty to bring you back into the Empire of the Seas where you belong."

"It will be a prosperous rule, just as it was under Cnut." The king's companion lifted his nose toward Ulf. "I am Tostig Godwinson."

Ulf knew the name Godwinson. It was the same name of the man claiming to be the king of England, the false claimant they sought to drive from the field.

"We are fortunate that the Jarl and his men have joined us," Hardrada said.

"Eighteen men will hardly make a difference in battle," Tostig said.

Amusement filled Hardrada's eyes. "Then you do not know the story of Ulf Bodvarsson and his Lochlainn. Fiercest berserker I've ever seen. Touched by Odin he is."

Tostig shifted uncomfortably in the saddle like he'd been plagued by a cluster of saddle sores.

"You are a brother to Harold? Cousin?"

"I am Lord Harold Godwinson's brother, but the true king has sworn to aid me in securing my lands."

Hardrada grinned at Tostig. "That I have. Look about you. This is yours. I will need competent men to rule in my stead once I've cut off Harold's manhood and fed it to the flames." He peered at the English lord. "If I can find it. Otherwise I will settle for his head on a spear."

Tostig appeared uncomfortable at the mention of his brother's demise but lowered his head in grace. "For that you have my undying loyalty, King. I swear to aid you in any endeavor you choose to take." He bowed in the saddle toward the king of Norway, and Hardrada ignored him, waving Ulf closer.

"I beg of you, Ulf, come and join me at my fire in the camp. We will share tales of long ago with a horn of mead, and we will enlighten Tostig to the will of the gods if he is brave enough to listen."

"I would take wine and meat after such a long journey from the Isles."

"Then come with me. We have much to speak of."

Hardrada and Tostig turned their mounts away from the bridge and began walking back to the camp. Ulf walked alongside the two men, his long strides keeping pace. Norse warriors ate, drank, and reveled in their recent victory. Men gambled with dice freely wagering gold taken from the defeated English warriors. Even wounded men smiled from beneath bandages and leaned on crutches, cradling injured limbs.

"I was unsure you would come on this campaign," Hardrada said. "You have been quiet for years."

"I do not seek battle as I once had."

"Your son?"

Ulf walked in silence for many strides before Hardrada spoke again. "I mean no insult."

"He is gone now. Nothing will change that. He always was an impatient man. Death tends to come to them quicker than others."

"For all the joys it brings, the Guard is a dangerous place."

"Many have fallen in service to the emperor."

"Uphold the Oath."

Ulf glanced upward at the king atop his mount. "Uphold the Oath." He had not spoken the motto of the Guard in some time. It was like meeting an old friend on his tongue. One that had known you for good and ill, but one you had not seen in far too long.

"You answering my call to war means much, brother. It has been too long since we have fought side by side in the shield wall."

"Crowfeeder's hunger is not easily satisfied." He brandished his long axe for Hardrada to view before he switched it to his other shoulder.

"May she feed well before the war is over."

Crowfeeder was a ruggedly elegant weapon that had been in his family for centuries. The grime of battle had been ground into the wood's very grain giving it a reddish-polished hue. Runes had been carved over the shaft telling tales of past owners' heroism. He ran a hand over it. Some of the runes were faint, worn away by the seawater and salty air, mere mists of memories. But his story had yet to be carved, a smooth section along the edge of the haft, condensing a man's deeds to a few runes was no easy task.

"Do you know where the English king is now?" Ulf asked. He had long known the people of these lands as Saxons and the term English felt foreign on his tongue.

Hooves galloped over the dirt road. Hardrada gestured southward. "My spies tell me he is hundreds of leagues to the south waiting on the Bastard of Normandy to come and assert his claim by the sword. His delay is our reward. We've defeated the ealdorman of Northumbria and his brother. A new sun rises upon my empire just as it had once before."

Ulf nodded. He knew intimately the longstanding tradition of controlling Jórvik as a base for waging war against the English to the south. He had been there the first time almost two hundred years earlier. "Jórvik will serve you well as it has many of our kind."

"The people welcomed us," Hardrada said with a laugh.

Flashes of slaughter filled Ulf's mind. They were not welcoming the first time, and they paid for their defiance in blood and tears, but he left those memories to himself.

"Welcomed their true lord," Tostig said from the other side of Hardrada.

"About as welcoming as the marshes to their men, Ran's net dragging them below by the dozen. You should have seen them sink after we broke their flank." Hardrada faced Tostig. "You *English* should learn to swim better if you're going to wear your armor in the waters."

"And you wouldn't have known their weak disposition without my counsel," Tostig retorted.

Hardrada's tone shifted to that of a man praising a loyal dog. "You have provided us with useful information and will continue to do so."

"I am a faithful servant."

"This land embraces us like a big-bosomed whore," Hardrada said.

"Green lands breed soft men," said Ulf.

Tostig held his tongue, rocking silently with his mount.

Ulf's ears caught the sound of hooves off the wooden planks of the bridge. All three men turned to look behind them. His keen eyes found the two crews of Norsemen over the river. Erik's pale body glistened as he grappled with a man rivaling his size. A raucous cheer erupted as he threw his opponent over his hip. As Erik let him regain his feet, the man lunged for Erik's legs, his opponent trying to hoist him upward at the knees. Erik brought an elbow into the man's shoulder and gripped his arm, bulling him backward to the ground. Another acclamation sounded off from the men. Coin traded palms in victory or defeat. Horns crashed together, and the men drank to a match well fought.

The two riders galloped onto the road from the bridge, one atop a sturdy red stallion, the other clearly a Norseman, atop a smaller mount. When they reached the three men, the riders drew to a halt.

"I bring a rider from Jórvik, my king," said the blond-bearded messenger. He bore no armor, only a simple tunic and a shining silver torc around his neck.

The emissary next to him had fierce blue eyes like an ocean squall, a long blond mustache stretching from his broad face. His cloak was red, and he wore a coat of silver mail. He had an unafraid glint to his eyes, and they settled upon Tostig with clear disdain.

Hardrada regarded him with curiosity. "Where are my hostages?"

The messenger's eyes hardened. "They will not be delivered this day or the next."

Hardrada laughed and glanced at Tostig. His comrade silently gulped. "You would break the terms? This does not bode well for your people or these lands."

"We have new terms."

"Should have known the dogs wouldn't keep their word. Honor is hard to find amongst cowards."

There was something familiar about the emissary in his voice or something in his eyes. He continued speaking, defiant, as if their presence repulsed him.

"You will leave these lands, or all your men will die here."

Hardrada laughed from his belly, his girth jiggling. "This man blows foul wind at me."

"We have only just begun to resist your invasion."

"What will you offer me leave this field? Look around you, lord. I have the only army here."

"I offer you what you are due."

"And what's that?" Hardrada asked.

"Your height in English soil."

Hardrada's mirth faded on his lips, an angry red dawn creeping onto his cheeks. "After I remove your head with my bare hands, I will let the ravens peck out your eyes and feast on your insolent flesh."

Ulf tightened his grip upon his long axe. "You best be careful, Englishman. You insult my friend."

The emissary turned on Ulf. His scent of fear was masked by anger on a sword's thin edge of violence. "It is meant that way."

"Then you shall soon become acquainted with Crowfeeder."

The emissary did not address him, only turned back to Hardrada. "You will leave now or suffer your fate."

"The Norns weave my fate, and they have fated me to rule these lands."

"Then your time here has come to an end," the emissary said.

Hardrada shook his head, jabbing a finger at him. "Who speaks to a king in such a way? Tell me your name so I can tell everyone what brave fool's skull I drink from."

"I am but a servant of England." He locked eyes with Hardrada before turning on Tostig. "There is no worse fate than a brother who raises arms against his own kin. May God forgive your sins."

Tostig paled, his voice soft. "I fight for what is rightfully mine."

"You turn your backside to the Norsemen when you should stand with your brethren." The emissary did not wait for a reply but turned his horse around and heeled its flanks. The red stallion whinnied spittle flying from its lips and swiftly moved into a gallop. Its hooves pounded off the wooden bridge before he disappeared into the forest of oak and birch leading west toward Jórvik.

Hardrada stared harshly at the forest before sharing a glance with Ulf. "I wouldn't mind putting a few more ealdormen into the ground." He shook his head at the thought.

"Call for the ships and the rest of your men," Ulf said. "Defeated men do not speak in such terms unless they want to die fighting."

"Nonsense. A few men seek the afterlife from behind city walls." He turned toward Tostig whose eyes were transfixed upon the road. "What say you? Who was that brave fool?"

Tostig gulped, his throat moving slowly before he spoke. "That was my brother."

"Brother? Which one?"

"King Harold Godwinson."

Hardrada's brow furrowed. "Impossible. He is fifty leagues away."

Tostig shook his head tersely, wiping a glistening sheen from his brow. "I know my kin. It was him."

Each man watched the forest road where Harold had disappeared with the intensity of a man hunted by hounds. Heartbeats disappeared into the sands of time. From across the river came the bellow of a horn followed by the sound of spears banging rhythmically off shields. The sound rising in intensity with every passing breath, forcing a snarl onto Ulf's lips. "The enemy comes."

II

Shadowed forms emerged from the forest road at the run. When the sunlight struck their mail, it reflected the sun in a blinding glare. The armored men held round shields painted red, white, gold, and black. Some were plain unpainted covered in tan, white and brown hide, some were constructed with a metal boss at the center, others without it. As one, they raced over the short distance from the trees toward the two crews of Norsemen guarding the bridge.

"God help us," said Tostig. He quickly made the sign of the cross over his chest.

The corner of Hardrada's mouth twitched as more armored men emerged from the forest. A standard-bearer bore a banner with the yellow wyvern upon a field of red. "Wessex's symbol. How can he have gotten so close with no warning," he growled at Tostig.

"I do not know, my lord. My spies all told me he waits for William in Wessex."

Hardrada leaned over the horse and grasped Tostig's tunic, crumpling it in his fist. "If you survive this, I want all their heads." He released Tostig and the Godwinson brother straightened his tunic.

The Norsemen across the river rushed for shields and weapons. They scrambled to form a small shield wall as the first English warriors crashed into them, but what started as a few men hacking and slashing, blades biting over and under shields, quickly turned into hundreds. Ulf could make out Erik's fiery braided beard dangling over his bare chest, his armor and tunic discarded to wrestle.

"Our men will purchase us time. They must," Hardrada said.

"It will not be enough." Ulf peered backward at the encampment. The warriors along the outskirts stared into the distance. The pounding of swords and spears on shields intensified as more warriors flooded from the forest.

"Those men cannot be saved," Ulf said. He pointed back toward the camp. "Rally your army, Hardrada, the English draw near."

Harald bellowed in a rage, spittle flying from his lips as he drew his sword. "Come, Tostig. We have more *English* yet to kill." Both men began to ride for the camp while Ulf donned his rounded-eyepiece helm, straightening it as to not impede his vision as he marched for the bridge. Crowfeeder was light in his hands, a simple stick, not the heavy-headed long axe that it was in reality.

The Norse crews were driven rearward by the sheer weight of the English numbers. Norsemen bled from every slash, jab, and strike not deflected by their shields. The wounded fell, lifting arms to shield themselves, and were trampled beneath English feet, spears, and swords in vengeful hands rising and falling on the defeated. The army needed more time, and Ulf would give it.

Hardrada turned his horse abruptly as he realized Ulf did not follow. He urged Ulf to his side with his sword. "You delay?"

"Go to your men," Ulf said.

Tostig leaned closer to Hardrada. "King, we must make for the camp before we are caught in the open."

"Away, woman," Hardrada said, his eyes falling back upon his old friend. His brow furrowed. "You go to meet your ancestors?"

"I have men across the river. I am sworn to them as you are to yours."

Hardrada's upper lip lifted in a snarl. "The skalds will sing songs of your deeds. We will feast and war together in Valhalla. Die well this day, Ulf Bodvarsson. Your ancestors and the gods watch." Harald saluted by slamming the pommel of his sword into his chest, and he turned his horse back toward the camp, shouting at men as he rode. "Raise the Landwaster! Let them know what fate awaits them here."

Norse blood flowed, and Ulf never looked behind him. He sprinted for the ships, bending near a fire to grab a flaming log. Wielding it as a torch, he crouched among the ships ensuring each caught flame before moving to the next. It made him sick to burn such fine craftsmanship but there would be no men to crew them if they did not prevail here. Soon a cloud of black smoke and crackling flames accompanied the pounding of English shields and the cries of the Norse as they were felled across the river. He moved along until he reached his own ship.

Old Floki untied a rope with the help of the youngest member of the crew, Uri. Both men stood silent, waiting for orders. Ulf shook his head.

"We will lose her if she stays here," said Floki.

Ulf scanned the forested field. More Englishmen gave a battle cry as they charged toward the crews, shields smashing into the backs of men in front, adding more weight to the shield wall. The Norsemen retreated faster, struggling to maintain any sort of cohesion. Time slipped away from them. Soon they would break and be slaughtered where they stood.

He swung his axe through the rope then raced to the other side of the longship, pointing at old Floki. "You were a steersman once. Guide the *Sea Raven* back to Riccall and warn Orri. He and his host are needed in all haste. The current will take you quick enough. You only need guide her." He turned to Uri. "Aid him."

"What of the crew?" asked Uri.

"Get on an oar, lad," Ulf commanded.

Floki hollered at him as he walked along the center beam. "Help me disembark." He found the steering oar and slid it through a loop of rope, settling it into its brace at the rear of the longship.

Uri hefted an oar waist-high as if he meant to use it against the English.

"Hurry, lad. You will meet them again," Floki said. Sweat beaded on his skull as he prepped the ship; he used his sleeve to wipe it away. Uri moved to the side of the ship and jammed the oar into the muddy bank of the river. He grunted with effort, the pinewood oar bending under the pressure.

Ulf lowered a shoulder into the ship's hull. His shoulders and legs tensed as the longship resisted him, refusing to release from the mud's embrace. His feet sunk deeper with every renewed effort. Yet he would not be deterred. Veins swelled in his neck and arms. He strained, and step by step, the ship eased into the water, the load lightening as the water accepted her.

The current tugged at the rear of the longship, straightening her. Ulf waded into the river, pushing the ship further into the current. Floki leaned on the rudder to avoid the burning cluster of longships, Uri laboring under his oar to keep them away from the flames until the *Sea Raven* was in the center of the river.

Floki gave a sullen nod toward Ulf. He turned away, stooping lower in the ship. He pressed his girth into the steering oar. He raised a fist in salute. The English flooded along the riverbank, but they would not dare try to swim to the opposing side. Unable to reach the retreating Norsemen, they jeered the fleeing longship. Smoke obscured them, faceless warriors caught in the rush of battle.

A towering warrior waded into the muddy waters. A frown spread on Ulf's lips as he watched the warrior. He bore a conical helm, with dangling ear pieces, long golden hair hanging from the below the helm. His shining mail marked him as an elite amongst their enemy. He carried a great bow in his hands as long as a man was tall.

He stretched the bowstring back toward his ear with ease as if the massive bow were a toy. He turned the bow skyward. The bowstring thrummed. Ulf followed the arrow as it arched in the sky then glided downward like a hawk diving for prey. With a thunk, it crunched through Uri's chest and punched out his back. The strike was like a vengeful Thor had thrown his beloved hammer, Mjolnir, spraying lightning in arrow form. Uri gaped in disbelief before toppling over the side of the *Sea Raven* into the river.

Ulf snarled in disgust. "You!" He pointed his long axe across the river. "Crowfeeder will taste your blood this day."

The archer turned his way. Deep scars defiled his shadowed face. Blue eyes peered from beneath his helm. His fingers grasped the feathered arrows in his quiver as he selected his next arrow. Something twinged at Ulf's nose. Something familiar. A primal stench. He let out a growl, shifting his shield from his back to his arm. The archer drew, and Ulf made himself a smaller target. Then the arrow came for him. He shifted his shield overhead and the arrow crashed through hide and wood.

Ulf scrambled over the embankment and jogged for the crossing. He weaved through a copse of trees to conceal himself from the archer. English voices shouting carried over the river. An arrow quivered as it hit the tree behind him. He did not slow. He could see what he thought was Erik's pale naked torso battling with urgency, weapon darting over and under his shield. He thought maybe Halfdan was with him. The chaos of battle made men hard to tell apart. No sign of Knud.

The bridge materialized through the smoke. It was of simple construction spanning the river at its shortest point. Tresses and beams supported the sturdy crossing that could withstand the current. It could fit no more than three men across at once or one man with a single cart. Ulf did not know if another ford or bridge resided nearby, but if Harold's army sought to risk a crossing here, it must be far.

A horn bellowed from Hardrada's encampment. Warriors hurried to form a shield wall in fits and starts, groups of men rushing to organize, almost all armorless save for shields. He could make out the king, sword circling overhead, as he urged them to hurry.

They headed for a small ridge, the elevation only enough to make it worth utilizing, in front of the camp. Hardrada was a war leader. He understood the advantage terrain could bring, and he sought to maximize what little advantage this land had to offer his armorless men.

Ulf would do the same. The bridge could make one man into a hundred, and he would make them take it from him piece by bloody piece. He sprinted toward the Norsemen dying on the west bank, his feet striking the bridge with hollow thumps.

"Lochlainn! To me!" he screamed over the din.

Hearing the call, Erik glanced over his shoulder before thrusting his sword at an Englishman. Only a dozen Norsemen still stood in a tight line, they bled from countless wounds as they were mangled by the heavily armored huscarls of Harold. Halfdan staggered and dropped to a knee as a spear head and half a shaft stuck into his thigh.

Erik jabbed his sword into an Englishman's face, the warrior screaming as he held a ruined eye. He grabbed Halfdan, backstepping for the bridge. He covered them both with his shield. He turned a blow from a long axe with his shield boss, and he dodged a spear thrust from the other side. He slashed at a warrior in one direction then swung wildly at another shield before sending the sword point into the closest warrior's foot. The warrior groaned as Erik's sword sliced through shoe leather severing sinew and notching bones as it pierced him. He wrapped an arm around Halfdan, stumbling for the bridge.

The last remnants of the Norse crews were brought down and butchered. There would be no prisoners, at least not now. Erik dragged Halfdan for safety. Ulf planted his feet awaiting them on the edge of the bridge. He held his shield high on his forearm so he could defend himself from arrows and still wield Crowfeeder with both hands. Erik brushed past him carrying Halfdan, red cheeks puffing. Halfdan's leg bleeding and limp as they passed. The English hounded them like dogs.

"Odin owns you all!" His battle cry only faltered them a half-step before the English warriors sought to overrun him. Some lessons were only learned in blood.

A dirty stubble-faced huscarl charged, sword overhead. Blood splatter coated his ring-mail. Unlike much of the English host, his shield was in the shape of an almond, making it more effective on horseback. Ulf took a long step sideways, swinging his long axe simultaneously. Crowfeeder's edge swiped the man's leg clean through at the knee. Fresh blood splashed upon the bridge. The swordsman went down screaming, grasping what was left of his leg, and Ulf took a step rearward.

Another English warrior made for them, and Ulf bashed him with his shield. The warrior stared blankly, eyes unseeing, before Crowfeeder lodged into his neck and brought the man to his knees. Blood rained, dousing Ulf's scale armor and face with warmth. He centered a kick on his chest, sending the brave warrior to finish dying on his back. Another huscarl thrust with his spear and Ulf hacked the shaft in half. The warrior tried to stab at him with the spearhead, and Ulf hooked him with the beard of his axe, twisting his body to throw him into the river. The warrior's hands scraped the surface of the current, and he disappeared under its waters.

Erik had set Halfdan down on the other side of the bridge and rejoined him near the center of the river crossing, chest heaving. "My father did not lie when he said you were Odin touched." His pale flesh glistened with sweat mixing with blood. Slashes crisscrossed his body and arms. He held his sword in one hand, shield in the other, as he caught his breath.

Ulf glanced skyward. "May he guide my axe."

The northerners searched the enemy army with wide eyes, seeking the next Englishman to put to the sword and axe. But their enemies were not fools. They could see the bottleneck and the two determined warriors in their path with no way around. The English had no berserkers to match them. Those few wild, unleashable souls of the Norse, fearing neither the gods nor death.

The English were Christians. There were many armed men but few true warriors among them. They had no wish to die even if they would die in plenty when the whips of their king drove them to cross Ulf's path. Even many of the Norse were Christians, but along the fringe of the kingdom there were those who abided by the Old Ways. Men like Ulf and his Lochlainn who lived by a far more brutal code best suited for dark forests and distant islands.

"Knud?" Ulf asked.

"Took an axe to the skull."

Ulf nodded, eyes searching for their next enemy. "We will see him soon."

"Aye."

"The *Sea Raven* rides the river to Riccall."

"She deserves a better fate than this shallow Saxon stream."

"Agreed."

"We must buy Orri's men time to join us." Ulf glanced at Erik. The young man understood that they must die here.

"Then we shall dine on the bones of the English."

"We shall feast upon them," Ulf growled.

The English interlocked their shields, something unknown holding them from charging. Armored huscarls formed the center, almond-shaped shields painted with wyvern, boars, and crosses. They would be the first of the brave men to die before the two warriors on the bridge. Their ranks deepened as more of the English army gathered on the field. Thousands of men, most were poor farmers of the fyrd, trained by the household guards of the English lords to fight, holding spears and round hide shields, hearty enough to die with a battle cry. Others held hunting bows, seaxes, and woodsman axes.

The ranks of the English haphazardly parted as a small contingent of horsemen pushed their way to the front. The mounted warriors were finely armed. One of the riders bore a white standard. At the center was sewn the image of a helmed warrior holding a sword and shield, the product of hundreds of gold coins tied individually to the banner. The warrior's eyes were made from green stones, his sword tip covered in red stones. The weight of the metal on the fabric forced the man beneath to constantly shift the banner for it to remain displayed.

King Harold Godwinson was with the riders, dressed in a shining coat of mail with additional leather armor over the top, a red cloak around his shoulders. His long blond mustache stuck out from beneath his helmet. The helm's nose piece was gold. He peered at the bridge, as more of his men flooded from the forest road. His eyes found Ulf and Erik. He pointed at them with his sword, angrily speaking to a tall warrior alongside him.

"Perhaps we will kill a king this day," Erik said, his breath beginning to calm. He pounded his sword onto his shield. "Join us you whoresons! Meet your fathers."

"Long ago, I promised your grandfather to watch over his kin. To guide you on your path. He would be proud to see you now. You never back down from a fight. You're always one of the first to wet his sword. Your ancestors will be proud to see you soon."

"It gives me great joy to know the hour nears."

A lord yelled from along the edge of the river. A disorganized company of archers moved to the front of the battle line. A bow was a coward's weapon but he had seen it used with deadly enough purpose in the East.

"No man wishes to test his worth upon us?" Ulf shouted at them. "Does no man wish to lock blades with Jarl Ulf Bodvarsson of the Lochlainn? Is there no champion among you?"

The company of archers answered his call. Arrows arced through the air, a flock of gulls ascending. Ulf and Erik lifted their shields. He glanced at Halfdan sitting on the river's edge behind him. He sat on the ground, bent on his side to favor his wounded leg, holding his shield in anticipation.

Moments later the arrows came for them. Whispers of death before they thudded into the bridge and shields, the sound of metal rain striking wood. Their shields rocked with every arrow. The deadly rain eased, and Ulf glanced at Erik. A smile took shape on the red-bearded man's lips. "To die beneath a raven's sky is an honor to the gods."

The sky cleared of arrows and both warriors were unharmed. They lowered their arms, smashing arrow shafts from their shields.

Erik cupped his mouth as he taunted them. "I offer you a trip to see your God." He stepped forward and thrust his sword at the ranks of men. "Come! I promise your passing will be quick."

Every moment the enemy delayed gave Hardrada's army a chance to prepare for the coming blood-letting. If the English wanted to waste arrows and insults with them, Erik and Ulf would do it all day. He glanced behind him. Halfdan lay prone now, arrows bristling from his corpse. Ulf exhaled heavily. *May the Valkyries guide your spirit on swift wings before Hel knows you are slain.* He had no doubt that Halfdan would find his way to Valhalla.

Behind them, Hardrada's Landwaster flew above his battle line. The red banner proudly displayed Muninn, one of Odin's ravens. The Norse's battle line was positioned at the apex of the small ridge. Along the flanks, Hardrada's men still assembled from the encampment. Most wore nothing but their tunics and trousers, but all had shield and weapons. It must be enough.

He turned back toward the English forces. More continued to pour onto the field. Thousands of English warriors layered upon one another. There would be no retreat. Only one army would return home. Only a violent briefness remained before many threads were sheared free by the Norns.

Erik laughed at death without remorse. "Odin terrifies you, and I am Odin's wolf!" He stuck out his tongue and roared at them, holding his shield and sword in the air. His muscles flexed throughout his body as he embraced his battle fury. Spittle foamed at the corners of his mouth. "Meet death!"

There was a sickening crunch. A barbed arrowhead burst from Erik's neck, entering near the throat and blasting out the side closest to Ulf. Death blood, dark and bitter, cloaked Ulf's face. Erik tried to speak, a grotesque gurgle groaning from his lips. He stumbled backward into Ulf, gasping for air. He dropped his shield, hand reaching for the arrow, and Ulf eased him to the bridge.

He squeezed Erik's sword hand, pressing it tighter into his palm. Horns blew in the distance. More Norse formed a shield wall; warriors with spears were gathering on the edges to defend against a flanking attack by English horsemen.

"You hear that, Erik? The Valkyries sound their horns for another man enters Odin's hall this day."

Erik's eyes gaped, his chest heaving.

Ulf tightened his grip around the young man's sword hand. "They come for you, lad." Erik's hands squeezed the hilt tight. Ulf stared into his light blue eyes as the Valkyries took him, and his body fell to rest. "Tell your grandfather and father I will see them soon." Ulf gently rested the warrior onto the bridge. He stood tall, rolling his neck. The eyes of the enemy were upon him. He stretched his axe toward the sky. "Odin, give me strength." His chest rattled with the coming storm of battle. "Who among you seeks death? Send your champion."

After a few moments, a warrior walked forth from the shield wall. He hoisted his sword and shield over his head. Smoke swirled about them obscuring the man. The enemy warriors howled like wolves for their champion. The huscarls beat their shields in unison. Through the smoke, Ulf caught glimpses of King Harold's grin as he watched his army cheer his captain. The hero of the English hefted his shield, pointed his sword at Ulf, and jogged for the bridge.

III

The English champion halted near the edge of the bridge thirty paces from Ulf, his helm lowered, eyes shadowed, his mouth spread in a determined scowl. Wrinkles creased his weather-beaten face. Sweat glistened upon sunken cheeks, his long nose pushing against the guard of his helm. He loomed over Ulf by a head and a half, but he was lean, spread almost too thin but with a reach that could kill a man before he was close enough to be a threat.

His ring-mail hung above his knees, and a blue cloak was fastened with a silver horse head brooch. His shield was painted a shade of blue matching the sky on a clear day with a white horse's head in the center, anchored by a polished iron shield boss.

"The bravest Saxon here," Ulf called to him. "I was wondering which among you wished to die first."

The champion snorted his contempt.

"What do you call this place?"

"The locals name it Stamford Bridge."

"Is this the place you wish to fall? You wish the fish of these shallow waters to fill their bellies with your flesh? When they are through and your body washes ashore, you wish your bones to whiten in the sun here?" Ulf asked as he eyed the sun.

"Tell that to your men on this side of the river."

Ulf never let his gaze falter. "They died well. Odin will be pleased to have them in his hall."

The champion sneered, his voice coming in gruff tones. "They died licking the dung from our feet. Calling out for their whore mothers." He turned around and lifted his sword high in the air. "For King Harold! England! England!"

The English imposed a fearsome cheer to the heavens, banging weapons upon shields. The champion fed off their energy before he turned to face Ulf once more. "I'll use your beard to wipe my arse before we're through."

Ulf held his building rage in check. Once unleashed it would not be satisfied until the field was littered with corpses. It was the berserker's rage. The wrath of the wolf. The fury of the bear. Violent and uncontrollable, it was feared by mortal men regardless of which gods they worshipped or what creed they followed. Many would die and soon. "By what name do they call you?"

"I am Cedric of Mercia." He touched his sword to his chest. "Captain of Harold's personal guard." He leveled his gaze. "I been cutting down your filthy godless kind since I was a child."

"The sun sets on those days."

Cedric sneered through brown teeth. "God gives me the strength of a dozen men against the devil."

"I am far worse than your devil. You look well-practiced serving your *argr* god on your knees."

Cedric's mouth tightened with his insult. "Your torment will be eternal in Hell."

"You wish to know torment? Join me on the bridge."

Cedric raised his arms again toward his men. They cheered him, banging their weapons over shields, a cacophony of false battle before the real one began. He lifted his sword heavenward before leveling it over his shield, long strides taking him upon the bridge. His shoes thumped the wood with purpose.

The smoke from the longships engulfed the men in a swirl of black wind. The fires added heat to the swelter of the day, the smoke drying their skin even as sweat poured from them. Bearing his shield on his forearm, hands grasping Crowfeeder, Ulf waited for Cedric to close.

His control surprised Ulf. He assumed the man would charge him swinging wildly, the anger of battle taking him. That would have made the champion easier to cut down because of the narrow confines of the bridge. But this man showed prowess by maintaining control of his emotions. Sweat streaked Cedric's face, but his snarl never slackened. He lunged for Ulf, a yell escaping his throat. Shields smashed together, but it was Cedric who was forced back. He took another step and thrust with his sword once, twice, then swung it sideways, trying to catch Ulf in the neck.

Ulf deflected all three blows then ducked beneath a pause and slash. Cedric struck out with his shield twisting Ulf's to the side to create an opening, and jabbed with his sword. His reach was that of a spear. Narrowly avoiding the sword's point, Ulf shifted out of range. He half-swung at Cedric, the long axe bouncing off his shield's iron boss with a clang. A grin smeared Cedric's lips. His eyes told a story of a glorious victory. He thought he held the upper hand. Cedric whirled his sword over his shoulder back and forth, determined to beat Ulf onto his heels with the harshness of his blows.

Cedric's sword bit into Ulf's shield repeatedly, hewing pieces of wood from the edges, the blade snapping at him. They neared the center of the bridge, Ulf having been driven across. The champion gritted his teeth in determination, his chest rising and falling rapidly from his onslaught. Ulf waited for Cedric to start his advance before he swung his long axe overtop of his shield. The blow stunned the Mercian, dazing him for half a heartbeat. Ulf attacked again, his axe a blur of violence. Cedric relinquished a step. Crowfeeder performed her dastardly work, cutting the champion's shield to kindling, stripping it piece by piece. When barely a plank remained, the axe cut deep, and Cedric cried out. He tossed his shield's remains into the river, clutching his bleeding arm across his body.

Cedric regripped his sword handle and went on the offensive, crossing his sword in a flurry of attacks, the blade a silver haze. Each swing slicing for Ulf's head and neck. He sought desperately to dispatch Ulf. Yet with each swing, more of the champion's blood escaped from his body to the bridge, dripping into the river below. Ulf parried and shifted, his opponent's strikes slowing with each renewed attack.

By contrast, Crowfeeder was a feather in Ulf's hands. The axe sang softly, a metallic whisper for blood. Cedric retreated a step with his sword pointed outward as if the point could stop Ulf from advancing. The storm had only just begun for the Mercian.

Ulf jabbed at Cedric's face, the champion grunting as it forced him off balance. He swatted at the axe with his sword. Now Ulf hacked from shoulder to shoulder at Cedric, building ferocity with each pass, *Hræsvelgr's* winds battering a floundering ship at sea.

Cedric's long face strained as he concentrated, deflecting and dodging without his shield, but he was not a man accustomed to being overpowered. He stumbled on a fresh corpse, and Ulf's long axe swept downward into his thigh. A deep cleaving wound split his muscle and flesh apart, and the towering warrior collapsed on the bridge with a thump, grasping for his leg. His sword fell from his fingers, teetering on the bridge's edge before disappearing into the waters below. Ulf assumed a wide stance, standing over the fallen.

"God will see you fall this day," Cedric said, his voice wavering. His lifeblood flowed freely through his fingers that desperately pressed the torn flesh together through his trousers.

"Your god holds no power here." Crowfeeder glided through the warrior's neck, and Cedric the Mercian, champion of the English, joined the dead.

Ulf bent down, shaking Cedric's head from his helm. Grasping his hair, he held it on display to the enemy army. "This is the fate of any fool brave enough to set foot on this bridge." He tossed the head toward them. It thudded upon the ground and rolled toward the English before coming to rest, Cedric's face pointed toward them. Ulf motioned at them with his axe. "Crowfeeder hungers for the English. She wants to dine on king's blood this day."

He pointed his long axe at one warrior than another. Their ranks were motionless, courage stymied by the death of their champion. "You? Or you? Surely another wishes to dull my axe on their bones." His eyes found King Harold Godwinson. Ulf pointed his axe at him. His wide mouth had puckered in disgust at the death of his captain.

"And you, *king*? Dare you meet my axe?"

Harold drew his sword, leveling it in Ulf's direction. "Any man who slays him will be my captain. Cut him down!"

The wall of Englishmen surged forward, a herd of emboldened deer, and a wolfish smile settled on Ulf's lips. The first huscarl to set foot on the bridge had his head cleaved down the middle. He dropped face down unmoving. While the second warrior was swept off his feet, Ulf spun, swinging his axe wide, wrapping around the next warrior's shield, his axe slicing through his back. The man screamed, eyes widening in terror, and Ulf kicked him into the man behind, sending both to the ground.

The English piled upon one another, the narrowness of the bridge Ulf's greatest ally, save for the one-eyed father of the gods himself. The enemy warriors struggled over the bodies of the fallen to reach him. On the edge of the slain he waited. A swarm of spear jabs over his latest victims forced him to yield slippery ground.

A spearman stumbled seeking secure footing around the fallen. Fear reeked from his person. In a sudden burst of speed, Ulf made a downward strike, his axe breaking through collarbone all the way to his ribcage. The man stood suspended by the axe in his body, and in a final act of defiance, rammed his spear into Ulf's shoulder. He howled at the Englishman, but the man was already dead. Ulf shook his axe free as a swordsman leapt over the fallen, his blade clanging off the wooden haft of Crowfeeder.

The swordsman swiped in a maddening fury hoping that Ulf's would had rendered him vulnerable. Yet it had the opposite effect, even as he pushed down the pain, his battle-blood bubbled inside him. In a swoop, he left the swordsman grasping for his missing foot. His comrades struggled past him as he moaned in shock.

The next man scrambled over the wall of bodies and had his neck ripped out by the beard of Ulf's axe, only whitish sinew keeping his head attached to his shoulders. He dropped like a sack of coins from a window, thudding on the bridge. Ulf sprinted for them, thrusting his long axe into the shield of another man. He followed by smashing his shoulder into him, running the shaft of his axe into the man's nose; the warrior lost his footing and toppled into the water. Spearpoints reflected the sun as they darted for him. He twisted and dodged.

A trio of spearmen approached more cautiously, driving him toward the center of the bridge, their long reach keeping him at bay. They treated him as one does a bear, never allowing him close enough to kill. He battered at their spears in return until he was able to hack the spearpoint off one. The warrior stared at his broken shaft, a fatal mistake.

Using the man to block the warriors' spears, he rushed closer, and he wrapped the hook of his bearded axe head around the man's torso and ripped, entrails spilling upon the bridge like a waste pail thrown out a door in the night. The attack left Ulf's flank open, and the other spearman rammed his spear through Ulf's chest, puncturing his armor. Grabbing the haft, he wrested the spear away and swung his axe one-handed over his head and crashed the blunt end into the man, sending brain and bone airborne. The body fell off the side of the bridge knocking his comrade from his feet. Ulf eased the spear out of his chest, wet wood over flesh, finishing with a gasp.

The final spearman's mouth shook as he watched. "No, please. Mercy, lord," he muttered to Ulf. He held a hand outstretched, eyes begging.

Ulf flipped the spear in his palm and jammed it through the man's mouth with such force it exploded out the back of his skull. He stood panting for a moment, glaring at the enemy army from beneath his brow. The enemy halted, shields raised, eyes peering overtop shields, waiting for him to stagger and fall from his wounds. He could read it in their eyes. Smell it in their stink. They still held that bloody hope they wouldn't have to face him. That he inevitably would succumb to his wounds. And they were wrong.

The pain was gnawing, but it paled in comparison to the worst he'd been through. The number of times he had been impaled, hacked or slashed was too many to count. As long as his head stayed on his neck and his limbs on his body, he would survive as would any man with his particular disposition.

He placed his foot on the spearman's shoulder, grabbed the shaft and removed the spear. He howled as he threw it at the closest Englishman. The force of the spear ripped through his shield, penetrated his mail, and nestled into his chest. He teetered on the edge of the bridge before falling into the current.

Ulf hovered his long axe toward the closest man. "Try again." The warrior took a step backward. Shouts of "kill him" raged from the English line, and that warrior was pushed to the side, his place filled with another man whose name no one would remember. Ulf hooked his shield, prying it from his hand before crunching the point of his axe head into his throat, caving it into a bloody hole. "Crowfeeder sings for more!"

The crunch of an arrow imbedding itself into his shield answered. He ignored the archer on his flank, grasping an Englishman who slipped inside his guard. Ulf smashed his helm into the man's face, the Saxon's nose cracking into his skull. He bent low, his canines extending before tearing into the man's neck. Coppery warmth filled his mouth, the blood flowing over his lips. He chewed the raw flesh before spitting it into the river.

With wild eyes he awaited them. He was one with the wolf, a warrior in animal form. An arrow struck his shoulder, staggering him, the barb penetrating through it and pinning his arm to his chest. He bit at it with bared teeth. Another arrow quivered in his shield. He tore at the one in his shoulder, clenching it between his teeth before ripping it from his body. Another sprouted from his other arm.

He roared at the English hanging back, fear shrouding their faces like a visible stench. "You dare not face me in battle? Sheep. Mere sheep." Another arrow hit him in the thigh, and he hissed at them brandishing his axe. "Show yourself, coward." Movement on the riverbank caught his eye.

The archer walked along the riverside, closing the distance, bowstring taut. *I see you, weak man, who walks with the cowards.* He adjusted his shield, and the arrow buried itself into the wood. With a yell, an English warrior tried to surprise him on the bridge, and Ulf kicked him down before slamming his axe into his chest. A barb pierced Ulf's lung. He peered downward, his breath becoming labored. He roared as he snapped the haft in half.

Two more warriors charged him, and he fended them off, grasping one by his mail coat before tossing him into the river. The warrior flailed before he disappeared in the rapid current. The second warrior stuck a dagger into his side. Ulf growled as he punched the shaft of his axe into his face, sending the warrior stumbling. Ulf followed through with his axe and hewed his arm from his torso. The warrior fell upon the bodies of his death-kin, blood spurting, as he joined them.

Ulf took a knee. An arrow rocked his shield. He covered his head, and another slipped beneath the shield lodging into his calf. The archer was relentless in his distant assault. The decision he made now was not one of an impetuous man, but one he made with the wish to delay the advance of the enemy. If the gods chose to spare him, he would be in their debt. If they allowed him to fall, the English would remember this day with great sadness for their many dead. He went inward, deep into the recesses of his mind.

In the darkness of his inner cavern, two golden eyes glowed waiting. They moved slowly side to side as the creature paced. They were one with him and the same, man and beast together as two souls intertwined, two ancient trees having grown into one. It waited for its chance to emerge. A chance to ravage his enemies. A chance to hunt. *It is time.*

The golden eyes, two suns penetrating the blackness of night, grew larger until the brightness came for Ulf. He threw his head back as he ceded control to the primality inside him. There was no turning back. Once the wolf was released, its fury would burn forth akin to the dwarves' fiery forges in a land of ice. Nothing would stand before it without being consumed, just as if he let the wolf linger too long in the light of man, it would threaten to consume Ulf until he was gone.

He howled in the presence of the sun. It had no place here. A beast of his breed sought the moon, for that was his mother, the goddess whom he worshiped above all. He dropped Crowfeeder. Then he cut the ties securing his cuirass to his sides and removed his belt, bending and shaking off his coat of mail. He grunted as arrows snagged on it. His heart increased tempo. His canines extended further, lengthening to spearpoints as his jaw grew outward into a muzzle. His ears grew to points, and his blue eyes melted in a flash of molten gold.

His muscles began to thicken and harden with blood, in particular around the neck. His gray-brown beard became as hard as ring-mail as the fur linked all over his body. His stature continued to broaden, and soon he was taller than the tallest man by an arm's length. His fingers stretched as they turned into dagger-like claws. He chopped downward on the arrow shafts protruding from his body. The English warriors halted. Each man stood statuesque, eyes agape, prayers and curses escaping dumbfounded lips.

The man Ulf had become the wolf known to his kind as the *Gray King*. He roared at the enemy, gory saliva flying from his mouth, spreading his arms wide, claws out, fangs bared. *Now the hunt begins.*

IV

The herd's terror was an avalanche raging from the highest peak, almost overwhelming his senses. A thousand two-legs reeked of the bitter stench, a rotten odor washing over the warrior once known as Ulf Bodvarsson. Now he was known only by a tapestry of scents as the *Gray King*.

Yellow-fear dripped down their legs. Yelps of newborn pups and hamstrung calves escaped their lips. The two-legs were weak and soft of body. When they were struck by fear, they made even easier prey, a herd to be driven in their avidity to escape. Effortlessly they were brought down by the master of the hunt. He breathed in their fear, desiring more.

A wounded two-legs rolled himself off the bridge and into the water. Bubbles replaced his shadowed form. The Gray King bent down and clutched a leg from one of their fallen, his knife-like claws sinking into its soft pink flesh. Each two-leg in the herd crowded his neighbor for shelter. While many wore the hard silver-skin, most did not, making them easy prey. A herd of silver sheep. He hoisted the bloodied corpse into the air and heaved it toward their lines.

The corpse crashed into the shields of the two-legs knocking them backward into the ranks behind. They scrambled to escape their dead comrade. Those that stood their ground gaped in terror. He lifted his head and roared again. *It is time to thin the herd.*

The two-legs made no attempt to attack him. They were an army of leaves in fall, trembling before his war-wind, prepared to drop at any moment. The man inside the beast, Ulf, soothed the wolf's rage. This was all desired. *Let them try us.*

Time, while only a passing breeze to a wolfskin, was an iron collar to the two-legs. Yet he understood, even in this form, that preventing the enemy two-legs from crossing the rapid waters was his purpose in life and death. His ears twitched. A thunderous call rolled down the ridge from the rival two-legs. His battle-kin. Those he sought to protect. Their howl of praise made his wounds fade.

He growled as the mounted enemy leader drove through his herd. He was surrounded by his pack of silver-skin-clad two-legs all mounted. They held hand-fangs or long-claws. He despised the cold, hard weapons of the two-legs. The long-claws were most dangerous for their reach, limbs of the shade-givers tipped with harsh points. A hand-fang reflected the sun and could cut or impale. Like the Gray King's tooth and claw each could be deadly in their own way.

Their bestial servants they rode he knew as tall-legs. Fearful beasts, fast and skittish, slaves to the two-legs, long in face and limb. He had tasted their flesh many times.

The herd leader spun his hand-fang over his head. His voice was a cub howling underwater. His pack picked up the yips and whines. Long-claws were leveled in his direction and the herd ran for him. He licked his lips, salivating in anticipation for the encroaching clash.

The bridge creaked as the Gray King shifted his weight. He hunched into a position of power, his leg muscles building tension as he waited to unleash a wolf-fury only known to men in the grave or on the run. Their scent of determination would collapse before his savagery. As the two-legs closed on the bridge, he threw himself into the air, claws outstretched. They jabbed at him with their long-claws and hand-fangs the fear reeking off them as he passed, missing him completely.

He landed upon the ones in front, crushing them beneath his claws. Wood and silver-skin crunched under his weight, their bones snapping like dry twigs. Long-claws on his flanks pricked through his fur in his chest and sides, mixing his lifeblood with theirs.

Ruthlessly he swept their long-claws away, swiping along them he left a trail of blood and screams in every direction. He swung his other claw, dashing it across a two-legs's face. His shriek reminded the Gray King of a fat-belly from distant lands.

He wrapped his jaws around the soft flesh of another's throat and ripped it out. Only the weight of their corpses kept him grounded. Another two-legs planted his long-claw into his thigh with enough force to penetrate through the muscle. The Gray King's massive jaws snapped, hoisting the two-legs from his feet. He swung the two-legs sharply, and with a satisfying crack, it went limp. The body fell amongst the carnage. Some of the herd tried to escape him, and he pounced, hurling them to the ground, bodies twisting as he landed atop, muffled screams coming from the brutalized wounded unable to escape. *I will return to feast.*

A line of two-legs riding their servile beasts galloped through the herd. Long-claws were grasped in their hands, hand-fangs held in others. They all bore silver-skin. A flag flapped behind them. The Gray King's snarl grew, flesh tumbling from his mouth.

He roared at them. The eyes of the two-legs at the center of the formation went wide as he neared. The mount reared upon its hind legs kicking, and the Gray King spilled its entrails to the ground followed by the rider.

The rider next to him stuck a long-claw into the Gray King's belly, but the impact jolted him from the saddle of his servile beast. The Gray King cut another out of the saddle, and he ripped the head off the next, spitting the tough silver-skin from his mouth.

A dying tall-legs rolled upon its back piteously shrieking. The Gray King grasped at the long-claw protruding from his belly as more two-legs swarmed around him. Each hack and slash from the herd angered him. He swung wildly to keep them at bay. For each two-leg felled, another took its place. A feathered-fang hit his neck, penetrating deep into the muscle. Followed by more. Each bringing pain. He brought his arm upward to cover his face, knocking long-claws away.

He moved backward toward the bridge. The pain was a dull reminder in the form of the wolf, but the injuries were real. He could be slain. He had seen other wolfskin perish. He had taken the heads of rivals. He could not regrow lost limbs or perforated eyes. He smashed his claw atop a two-legs's head, shrinking him in death.

Feathered-fangs continued to find him, so many he resembled a thorn-back. The cheers of his battle-kin sounded out from the ridge behind him. The Gray King could hear his other, Ulf, inside him. He wanted back out. Control slipped from the beast. A hand-fang darted upward from underneath the bridge and into his foot, piercing his sole and out the top. He howled and lost his footing and crashed through the railings. His claw dragged over the wood, leaving deep gouges, until he grasped Ulf's shade-feller before falling into the rushing water.

The river swallowed him. He went under the surface to the shouts of the enemy two-legs. Long-claws splashed in the waters around him. The herd of two-legs sprinted across the bridge. The man inside wrested control, and the wolf, Gray King, disappeared into the flowing waters.

V

The water washed over him. It stung his countless wounds. A bloody haze squeezed his vision, and he could only manage to keep his head above the river in breathless intervals. He was tossed and turned around, spun and disoriented, his limbs smashing upon rocks.

His battered knuckles crunched into a stone, his arm twisting as his axe caught in a crevice, and Crowfeeder was twisted from his fingers. He spun into the current kicking his legs, but the river would not relent before slamming him into a rock. Pain stabbed through his back and into his hips. Arrow shafts snapped or were pushed further into his body as he tried to stay afloat. His fingers dragged along the algae-covered rock face, and he was forced beneath the water. He fought desperately to reach the surface once more, but he found his left arm was dead weight. He was weakening, an almost unfamiliar concept to him.

He kicked off a rock and breached the surface. Greedily, he sucked in air. A tree limb hung low off the embankment. He lunged for it and missed. He kept his legs bent and feet upward as he tried to minimize damage and gain enough purchase to escape the waters. The current shifted and took him around a bend, and his fingernails ripped off along the jagged exterior of a rock. He went under.

Water swirled over his head. The air tightened in this chest as he slapped at the waters to get above them. Another tree lay fallen ahead, jutting into the river. He swam for the embankment then braced himself for impact. With a thud, air escaped sharply from his chest, his fingers seeking a hold along the rough veins of bark. His legs tucked under, following the flow of the current. He tried to hoist himself atop the trunk, but the river held him in place with the current's grip always threatening to suck him below. He shuffled his hand slowly, until his feet scraped the muddy river bottom.

He lost his footing and clutched the trunk with his right hand for balance. He finally managed to gain traction, using the tree to brace himself until he could crawl up the grassy riverbank.

Long grass spilled over the top of the embankment. His fingers ran along the blades before he clenched a handful, using them to hoist himself upon the bed of green. Dense timber, almost impregnable to the naked eye, crowded the riverbank, the trees in a constant war for the soil with the rushing water. With a grunt, he rolled onto his back, his chest rapidly rising and falling.

After a few moments, he let his eyes crack open. Leaves played with the light, obscuring then rustling with a cool breeze, leaving flashes of brightness sneaking through the shade. He lay still, the chaos of battle quieting for a moment in his mind, staring at the blue sky between the trees. No sounds of weapons crashing together or cries of the dying. The only sound was the bubbling voice of the river, calming when it wasn't threatening you with a watery grave. This was as close to peace as a man could hope to find in this land. The only greater peace would be the pleasure of sharing it with a woman. He embraced the temporary tranquility promised by succumbing to his wounds only to be renewed once again by his assured time in Valhalla.

Time drifted. The sun shifted. Blood flowed. Then lessened. He knew not how long he laid in the grass before he lifted his head, glancing downward at his myriad of wounds. Watery crimson still flowed from the most grievous. While he had seen himself in worse condition after a battle, it was never settling to gaze upon the decimated remains of your own body. Yet he would heal from the butchery of battle that would kill a regular man for he was no common man; he was a wolfskin, an *Ulfhednar*, one of the few men who was born bound to the wolf and the wolf leashed to the man.

He took his right hand and felt the jagged edge of a broken arrow shaft in his neck. He explored it gingerly with his fingertips. Finding the base, he clenched his jaw as he dug his fingers into the wound and freed the arrowhead from his body. Pain seared through him as the barbs cut through his flesh, but with a final snag, he tugged it free. He caught his breath and studied the metal arrowhead.

It was shaped like a triangle. He wiped away the blood then twisted it in his fingers. There was a swirl of lighter metal coating the iron point. The skin on the pads of his fingers started to tingle then burn. He tossed the arrow to the side with a groan of disgust.

The arrowhead was made with silver, a poison to his kind. Large quantities could kill him if left inside his body long enough. He spat bloody phlegm and forced himself seated. He went through the excruciating process of removing the dozen arrows sticking from his body. Few were made with regular iron, some with blended silver. The archer must have changed over to silver once he embraced his wolf form.

Ulf paused for a moment. His enemy knew his kind's weakness. Surely no man would use silver for his arrow unless his purpose was to bring down an *Ulfhednar*. He must be even more cautious now for a man knew his weakness.

He brought a hand to the hole in his chest. The skin was a tattered sail in a storm. With the silver poisoning, it would be slow to heal. Easing himself onto his elbows, he crawled down to the muddy riverbank, leaving a bloody trail in his wake. He scooped mud and shoved it in his wound. It would reduce the blood flow and give his healing a chance to begin.

He repeated the process for his other wounds. Gore gaped from a hole through his foot. It too would heal in full, but it would be days before he could run again. He felt for his bone-hilt long dagger hanging from his belt and removed it, gripping it in his functioning hand. He gingerly cut the remains of his shoe off then ripped strips from his tunic and wrapped his foot, caking it with mud. With a dissatisfied grunt, he gritted his teeth, using an oak tree branch to steady himself as he stood. He leaned on the sturdy trunk for a minute catching his breath.

"You will not keep her," he grunted at the river. The river bubbled an almost harmless response. He cursed himself for losing Crowfeeder. A weapon as ancient as it was elegant was a more prized possession than most anything, including gold. It could not be reforged or replicated. It was one of a kind. Passed down from warrior to warrior. He could never face his ancestors in Valhalla knowing that he was responsible for its disappearance.

He tried to recognize any landmarks from his voyage aboard the *Sea Raven*. He examined the terrain for a moment, his eyes finding the river and the sun in the sky. He was on the eastern side. He knew that much. The midland was forested both to the north and south. He vaguely recalled the forests as his ship had rowed from Riccall, but many places looked the same in this soft land.

Using the trees to aid his agonizing walk, he limped among them, leaking a trail of blood behind that any man or beast could track with ease. He hugged the river's edge, knowing the oak, birch, and thick bouts of holly concealed him from the other side. He sought Crowfeeder along the shallows of the current, but his eyes often drifted to the opposing side searching for enemy scouts or warriors. He made painfully slow progress north toward the encampment of Hardrada and Tostig.

Painstakingly he made his way north. His eyes scanned the woodland ahead of him, seeking friend or foe. Instead he found a stag standing motionless in the distance as if it had been carved from stone by an ancient people long ago. Its mouth moved to the side as it chewed. Ulf stared at the great beast of the forest for a time. It knew him as a threat and sensing his injuries knew he was unable to act as such. Unhurried, the stag turned away, hooves striking the undergrowth. It would prove folly to spook the animal for fear of giving away his position.

He limped onward, eyes gazing at the flowing river. He must find Crowfeeder again. Then his ears caught the sound of a distant battle. The two armies clashed. Odin will see Hardrada prevail. He crept closer, the clang of metal with metal, the thud of shields deflecting blows, and the cries of the wounded and dying escalated with every step. A hazy gray smoke hung in the trees from the burning ships while the sun reflected the shimmering shadows far ahead. He weaved carefully through the trees, and his nose caught the stink of the recently deceased.

The undergrowth parted, giving way to the mound of a body. It was an elder warrior with more gray than brown in his beard. He wore a muddied mail coat, his helm nowhere to be found, a hand-axe between fingers. Ulf saw no apparent wounds. *Illness?*

He stepped cautiously over the corpse and lifted the man's face with his knife. Eyes like the surface of a calm sea stared. Around the warrior's neck was an amulet. Once it had been

Thor's Mjölnir, but it had been carved into the cross of Christ. *He is one of Hardrada's.* Ulf gently let him rest again. As he closed on the forest's edge, obscured shapes clashed in the distance. He stalked behind a large oak, resting a hand on its trunk and watching for an opening to rejoin the army.

The bridge where he had made his stand was ahead. The longships smoldered in a line, fires burning into embers on the shore. Black carrion birds already circled overhead, waiting for a victor to emerge above the bridge of kings. Ulf was surprised any of them could still fly after the feasting they had indulged since the last battle.

He grimaced at the sight. The trail of the corpses and wounded strewn over the ground revealed how the battle had unfolded. The Norse had been driven rearward, shifting like a rapidly moving river of the slain. On the ridge near the Norse encampment, the battle entered a new stage. There were few Norsemen still standing, their shield wall broken. They dwindled as they crumbled apart into small circles of armorless crews in a sea of vengeful Englishmen.

Yet the Norse nearest the forest wore armor that brightly reflected the sun. They were being bulled rearward by the English. Ulf gripped his knife. He would join them. Odin had seen him kill enough today to send a Valkyrie to collect his soul when a rival warrior finally sent him to the afterlife. Holding his knife in an overhand grip, he emerged from the forest shadows. There was no want for spears and shields among the dead. He would stand shoulder to shoulder with the last of the Norse.

Then something caught his eye from the river's edge. Diminished silver reflected the sunlight like a fish in the depths. He glanced toward it. In the shallows, something metal lay. *It must be.* He hobbled over to the embankment, through black smoke and past smoldering ships, back crouched. *It must be.*

He grunted as he slipped down the riverbank, falling on his arse. He sheathed his knife and waded into the water, resisting the current. He raked his fingers over the riverbed and missed once before his fingertips touched the carved shaft of his long axe. His hand tightened around her even as the river threatened to steal her away once more. He heaved it free of the mud, clutching Crowfeeder in his hands. He marveled at the weapon as savage as it was ancient. His hand ran along the runes as he wicked away the droplets. "Nothing is lost that wants to be found," he said with a grin.

He used the axe as a crutch, shoving it into the ground to aid him over the riverbank. The sound of hooves echoing off the bridge hastened him to seek cover among the ruined ships. He crouched lower, groaning as he hid behind a burning hull. English riders walked their horses along the bridge. As they came on the western side of the river crossing, they broke into a gallop with a shout, completely focused on the battle ahead of them.

The horsemen raced toward the armored Norse flank, spears flashing in overhand jabs at heads and necks. The Norsemen were cut down where they stood. A few simply collapsed in the field and were butchered in their prostrated state. The Norse battle line crumbled.

Those that could run took flight. Warriors tossed down their helms and shields as they turned their backs and made for the trees. It was a sure way to die. Then again, so was standing their ground. Yet one held honor, the other clung to the lie of life. They were hounded by Englishmen on horses. They hacked them down as they fled. Ulf moved that direction, staying low in the long grass that hadn't been trampled leading back to the forest.

He watched as a horseman impaled a Norseman in the back then circled his mount around to get his spear. Ulf snuck along his flank. The warrior bent out of the saddle to retrieve his spear, and Ulf growled as he emerged from the grass. With a vicious one-handed swing, his axe cut into the warrior's arm. He screamed and fell from his horse. Ulf didn't bother with him again, moving once more for the cover of the trees and the trickle of defeated Norsemen.

He wrapped an arm around a fleeing Norseman, helping him into the edge of the forest. He carried the young man to the nearest tree and set him on the other side. He peered outward at the forest's fringe. Few Norse reached its borders. The horsemen circled back for easier prey, slaughtering any stragglers still trying to escape the field.

The young warrior sat with his back against the oak. Ragged breaths escaped his lips. A short blond beard attempted to take root on his face. He would have been better off shaving it clean than pretending to be a grown man. He leaned to the side to peer back at the battle.

Ulf took a knee in front of him in a position he could easily see any danger from the forest's edge. "What is your name?"

"Esmer Dagson."

"Has Orri come? Is this all the men from the ships?"

Esmer's eyes were wide, his cheeks redder than the blood that dribbled from the wound on his scalp. battle-wind was so fierce, the young man leaned forward and vomited. Ulf hoisted him standing. "Breathe, boy." His eyes tried to find the answer. "Were you with Orri's men?"

"We were beaten before we took the field." He coughed harshly. "Our warriors collapsed in their armor before they even fought a single Englishman. Orri led them into the English rear, but he was a storm of dying winds. He died bravely with any man that could still stand."

Ulf squinted around the tree as a man screamed on the forest's edge. A horseman stood over a facedown Norseman, spear in his back. The Englishman grasped the shaft of his spear with a dark look in Ulf's direction. Then he turned his mount back toward another running warrior. Ulf tried to see the fading vestiges of the battle. The fighting grew dimmer like the coming night.

"I don't see Landwaster. Has the king fallen?"

"He was already dead when we arrived. Arrow to the throat."

Ulf lowered his eyes momentarily. Hardrada was a fine man. Brave beyond measure. A worthy king. He doubted he would see the likes of him again for some time unless he too fell here this day. "Stay here. I must see for myself." Esmer slid down the trunk until he was seated once again. Ulf moved from tree to tree as quickly as his injured foot would allow.

He knelt behind a cluster of holly trees and watched the field. A pocket of men yet fought on, but the battle was breathing its last, and the English would carry the day. The wounded dragged weapons and damaged bodies back toward the bridge like bleeding *draugr*, struggling over the terrain. The last band of Norse fought to the last man.

The warriors were felled in heaps until one man stood alone before the English horde. He slashed and dashed. A spear found him and he yelled defiantly at his attackers. They impaled him with two more spears and brought him to his knees. An English sword severed his head from his neck in two powerful strokes.

The sounds of battle dispersed into history. A host of exhausted cheering expelled from raw throats and lucky souls. The English banged their weapons off shields in a clamor fit to call down the gods' fury. The horsemen pursuing the fleeing warriors turned their mounts toward the main army, spears and swords raised in salute. The Fighting Man banner of Godwinson was hefted high, the wind wrestling with it, the gems sparkling in the sunlight.

As one mass, the English army limped down the slopes of the encampment. Warriors dragged their weapons behind in wounded exhaustion. They stopped to loot the dead Norsemen, stripping them of all wealth: rings, necklaces, mail, and weapons. The still living Norse were put to the spear and sword.

Renewed cheers were roused as the body of King Harald Sigurdsson, known as Hardrada, was found surrounded by a pile of his foes. His limp body shook as it was stripped of all wealth, sword and shield, then hoisted onto the backs of the victorious Englishmen to be paraded for all to see. His body jostled with his captors, an arrow embedded in his neck, a dozen grisly wounds fiercely decorating his chest.

We will meet again, battle-brother, in the halls of Valhalla.

King Harold Godwinson rode next to them, hand outstretched as he acknowledged the praise of his warriors. His mount was covered from head to foot in blood and muck, the rider himself almost as soiled. His standard-bearer hefted the Fighting Man banner high.

Godwinson stopped for a moment, talking to some of his warrior-kin, his huscarls. His champions leaned from the saddle gripping arms with the dismounted men. One of his personal guards handed the king a spear, a head planted on the point. The English king hovered it close to his face, staring into the dead man's eyes. Then he hoisted the head for all to see. Jeers sounded from his men, but they were quieted by his booming voice.

"You would all see Tostig as a traitor, but I only see him as my brother, however misguided he was. I offered him a place by my side, and he rejected the noble forgiveness of a brother and his rightful king. He has paid the eternal price, and I will not hear his name defiled without punishment." His men quieted down in earnest reflection. Harold's voice throttled the crowd as it grew into a roar. "But the one they call Hardrada fell before English might!" He lifted the spear higher, and his men roared. After a moment, he let the spear fall to his side. "We have won a great victory this day. One that will be remembered in England for millennia to come as it was God's will. We will never forget the fallen for they paid for our lands and freedom with their blood. May Christ comfort their souls."

The king lowered his eyes. A priest came forward holding a staff bearing the cross. The Englishmen all knelt where they stood, knees squishing into the mud and gore. The priest chanted a blessing upon them and the dead.

Ulf scanned the field and bridge. Floki could not have made such a long distance on foot. Surely he stayed with the ships near Riccall. *We may be able to reach him.* He skulked back toward the base of Esmer's tree. He half-expected the young warrior to be gone, but the youth was still there catching his breath. Ulf offered him a hand off the ground. "We make for the ships in Riccall."

Esmer accepted his hand. "I've already run so far."

"You have no choice. It is make the walk or die here with the others."

"We will be branded cowards for not dying here," Esmer said as he stumbled behind Ulf.

"Says the man hiding in the forest. No. Our battle is done. The gods have collected enough of our battle-kin for Valhalla this day. I cannot speak for your favor before the gods, but perhaps the Norns will spin you more time."

The youth looked down at his feet. When his eyes leveled upon Ulf's, his cheek twitched. "You ran like me, old warrior. We are cursed."

Ulf threw a hand into his chest, stopping the young man. He inched his face closer, growling, "I was the man on the bridge."

The young man's eyes darted away, and he started to shake. "The bea-beast."

"It is me. Ulf Bodvarsson, the berserker, the *Ulfhednar*. I do not run from the enemy."

The young man's eyes darted to either side. "I meant no disrespect, my lord."

"Come. Your fate has brought you here. Let us return to the ships." Ulf released him and walked southward away from the field. By the soft boot tread, he knew Esmer trailed behind.

Before they'd gone two ship lengths, a terrible sound of ripping fabric cut through the air. It was closely followed by an explosion of blood onto the back of Ulf. He hefted his long axe and crouched. Esmer, a step behind, gaped, his jaw dropping, a triangle arrowhead protruding from his chest. Ulf grasped the man by the shoulders, shuffling him behind a tree, and leaned him against the trunk.

Esmer gurgled and spat, his head bobbing, as he choked to death on his own blood. He squeezed at the arrowhead, but it would have no effect. He would die here, feathered the same as a deer in the forest.

Ulf pried one of Esmer's hands from the arrow shaft. The young man fought him. "You need a weapon, warrior, or your fate will be worse than dying itself." He wondered if this man had even a chance to be chosen by Odin or Freya to join them in their valorous warrior halls. The man's hand leapt back to his chest, and Ulf pried it away and shoved the hilt of his sword into it. "Take the sword, boy. Only those who have reason to fear, fear death." He forced the young warrior's hand around the hilt.

Esmer noisily choked to death on his own blood. A twig cracked nearby, and Ulf placed a hand over Esmer's mouth. "Die quiet now," he whispered. He gradually edged away from the tree. The silhouette of a man aiming a bow filled his vision. An arrow splintered the bark, spraying wood fragments as Ulf ducked.

He turned away then pressed his back against the tree. He would have to move fast on the archer. He could only take so many arrows in his weakened state. If this was indeed the same archer, he'd have a fight on his hands. If he had more warriors with him, it may be Ulf holding the axe as he died before he joined Hardrada and his army in the next life. *Do not shy away from fate.*

He spun off the tree, hoisting his axe, making for the spot the bowman once stood. He quickly realized the enemy was no longer there. He slowed. *Sssippp.* An arrow hit his unprotected flank, and he flinched, turning in that direction. Another arrow was nocked in a blur of practiced movement. Ulf roared at him. He threw himself flat on the ground. A heartbeat later, a flash of fletching fluttered overhead.

Using the undergrowth to mask his movements, he rolled to a tree holding his axe close to his chest. He snapped the arrow sticking from his side. He waited a moment before he tossed the shaft in the air. An arrowhead hit the shaft, and both flew to the side. Ulf ran as fast as he could in the other direction. He could feel the man aiming at him before he took cover again. His wound began to heat, a gradual increase in fiery pressure. *Silver. Bastard.*

Ulf hunkered down low, letting his body hit the ground. He crawled away from the tree, green undergrowth masking his movements. His hands grasped for a stone, his fingers securing one in his palm. He listened for movement. Airy footsteps sounded over the leaves. A twig cracked. Ulf caught sight of the archer, a long bow flexing in his hands.

Slowly he pushed through the ferns and shrubs in the opposing direction. Ulf heaved the stone far to the right. The bowman aimed at the shaking ferns, but he did not loose. An Englishman on horseback crashed through the undergrowth. The archer spun on him and lowered his long bow a fraction, letting the arrow and bowstring rest easy.

The horseman raised a hand in defense. He wore a dull gray coat of mail and a red cloak secured with a white painted brooch of a lion. His blond mustache was cut short on a youthful face. "It is I, Ealdorman Leofwine. Do not shoot."

"I can see it is you, my lord." There was a hint of disappointment in the archer's voice.

"Then lower your bow, Arnulf. The battle is won."

Ulf inched his battered body through the greenery.

"I hunt a dangerous prey. A warrior among them evades my bow."

Leofwine scanned the forest. "Do more of the invaders lurk?"

"There is one that must be slain this day."

"They will never make it back to Riccall. Ealdorman Morcar and his remaining men have retaken their camp. If your prey reach Riccall, Morcar will be there to enact his revenge for his loss at Fulord. I assure you there is nothing he would like more."

"I would have this man's head. It is a feud of personal nature."

A short grin captured Leofwine's face. "Come. Join us in celebration. There will be a feast greater than we have ever known this very night. Harold has secured his throne. England is saved."

"I will return when I am through, my lord?"

Leofwine's grin saddened. "Let a few make it back to their lands so they can tell of our terrifying deeds."

Arnulf bowed his head. "I only ask that you let me kill this man."

"I will see you at my table later with the rest of my huscarls."

"Thank you, my lord."

"With men such as yourself, England will stand for a millennia." Leofwine turned his horse around, leading it back to the battlefield.

Arnulf turned toward the trees where Ulf had been. His eyes narrowed at his surroundings knowing Ulf still lurked. His intelligent eyes quickly scoured the forest, seeking signs of his prey. He upturned his nose, testing the air as he took light steps. The archer's scent had caught Ulf's again in the wind. It was familiar, akin to a distant relative, a smell that brought a grimace to his lips.

Arnulf stepped closer, and Ulf tensed, heart thundering in his chest. Arnulf stopped, the only sound the tightening of his bowstring. He drew his arrow back to his ear, holding the bow taut, displaying great strength. "Reveal yourself, heathen. I know you hide near." Ulf was silent, watching him through the leaves and brush. "Your kind usually have the honor of dying on their feet." He moved his aim over the trees and loosed. The arrow thudded into the vegetation ten paces from Ulf.

The archer began to stalk again. His steps were almost soundless through the foliage. A common man would not realize he was being hunted before it was too late, but Ulf was no such man. He was *Ulfhednar*.

As Arnulf passed his hiding place, Ulf rose from the vegetation as quiet and as slow as an oak, axe held in both hands, lip twitching in anger.

VI

Brush was trampled underfoot. The archer startled as he turned, lifting his long bow. Ulf threw his weight into a crushing blow. Crowfeeder hissed as she cleaved the air. The archer's movements were reactive but quick, and his arrow slipped away errantly into the trees as he hurried, his bow rising to deflect the axe.

The bow caught Ulf's swing in the center, and the bow snapped into kindling. Arnulf dropped the two pieces and threw himself backward, falling into the vegetation. Ulf followed, a step slow on his injured foot.

Rolling, the archer leapt onto his feet, a long seax in his hand. Ulf was undeterred, viciously attacking. He swung a wide arc, and the archer dodged, leaning desperately rearward to avoid a head-splitting blow. They repeated this game of kill or be killed until the archer backed into a tree. The misstep gave Ulf the time to bring his axe across his body in a backswing.

The blunt end of the long axe thumped off the archer's skull. He cried out as he collapsed into the undergrowth, rolled, and laid still. Ulf kicked the seax away from his fingertips. He placed the axe's edge against the archer's neck waiting for him to emerge from his darkness.

He rested heavily upon his uninjured leg, catching his breath. It had been many years since he'd been so tested by an individual warrior and an archer at that. Most warriors fought in close quarters with shields, swords, axes and spears. It was rare to face a warrior who wielded a bow in such a ferocious manner, especially off the battlefield. Vengeance was but only a matter of pressing the axe harder into his throat. But his hand stayed level, granting his enemy life for a short while longer.

After a few moments, the archer regained consciousness, his eyes blinking before narrowing. His voice came sudden and angry. "I do not fear death, heathen."

"If I were a younger man, I would have already taken your head."

"What stays your hand?" The archer pushed his throat into the axe's sharpness, the indentation in his skin threatening to cut. "If it were I standing over you, I would not hesitate to end your life, along with any man who names himself Norse or Dane."

"Stand," Ulf commanded. He relinquished the edge of his axe a fraction, allowing Arnulf the freedom to regain his feet. Using the tree to brace himself, the archer stood. His eyes darted as he sought a way to escape. "Why do you wait?"

Ulf's nostrils flared as he took in the other man's scent. He was sure of it now. He knew the secret lurking inside him. He'd killed wolfskins in the past, but he held his long axe in place. "You know the answer. Why do you want me dead?"

"I would rid this island of all your kind."

Ulf leaned closer and the man held his gaze. "But you and me are kin."

"I share nothing with you."

"We are both wolfskins. You know this." He touched the side of his nose. "You must recognize my scent."

The archer spat on the ground. "Then we only share one thing. If you have honor, finish this quick so that I may go be with God." The archer leaned into the axe.

Ulf gave no ground to Arnulf through the threat of self-demise. "Does life plague you so deeply that you are eager to die?"

The archer scowled, stiff pink scars on his face wrinkling. "There is naught else for me."

"Where is your family? There must be more like you?"

"They are dead and gone." The archer's face twisted at the word gone. "Now do it. Or I will call for the huscarls, and we will begin the hunt anew." His eyes barbed at Ulf. "And I will not show you mercy."

"That would only lead to more dead Saxons."

"We're English. But one less Norseman would defile these lands."

"You are too young to know anything else." Ulf lifted his axe head away from the archer's throat. "Join me, Arnulf. I have a place for men such as us far to the north."

"I would rather burn in the fiery depths of Hell."

"Yet you do not raise the alarm," Ulf said, allowing his axe to rest easy upon the ground. The two men stared at one another, blood feeding the green plants between them. "There are worse men than me in these very lands." Arnulf's eyes widened at the word. "You know the men I speak of." Ulf bent down and grabbed the seax's handle. He flipped the blade into his palm and handed it hilt first to the archer, eyes searching him for continued hostility.

The archer gulped, and he took the broad knife into his hand. "I know the warriors you speak of. They ride beneath the stag and cross."

"Aye. Then you know they pose a danger to us."

"I do." Arnulf slowly sheathed the seax. "It matters not. I have obligations to King Harold Godwinson. I am a loyal man to one of his lords."

"You know what they would do if they discovered your secret. Loyal huscarl or not."

Arnulf gulped. "I do."

"Then let me join you."

Arnulf sneered with a short laugh. "We would never take a man such as yourself into our army."

"Half the blood in your army comes from the Danes and Norse. Harold would take every Norseman he could find to replenish his losses this day. Your lands are not free from threat."

Arnulf did not look convinced even if he knew the truth of Ulf's words. He turned away and carefully collected the pieces of his bow.

"If the Norman bastard William comes, Harold will need every warrior he can find. Rollo's bloodline is strong, bastard or not."

"You would betray your army? Your men? Your king?"

"Betray? No. That army is gone. My men are dead. My oath to the Hardrada died when the last of his lifeblood fed the soil. I would join with my fellow wolfskin. We are few, and the many would see us destroyed. If they knew, they would kill you for it."

Arnulf clenched his jaw. "They would never learn it. I refuse to embrace it as you did in broad daylight."

"Every secret finds a way to the light. You must have wolf-brothers, or this world will snuff out your flame. I am surprised you have survived this long without them."

"And I welcome the end from this torment."

Ulf shook his head. "Then I name you lost. You will fall to the Wilds before long. Then no man can name you friend." He turned away using his long axe as a crutch to begin the long trek. He would head for the coast, seek passage back to his island. His footsteps crunched uneven and heavily through the undergrowth.

"Wait," said Arnulf. He held the pieces of the bow in his hands.

Ulf turned to look at him over his shoulder.

The archer's mouth twisted as if he'd eaten a rotten apple. "I would speak more of our bond. It has been so long that I can hardly remember my wolf-kin. My father." He gulped. "I can summon almost nothing of him. But the man who stole them all from me. I can remember everything. His eyes. The hook of his nose. The shape of his face. Every single hair atop his head."

"Tell me more of this treacherous man."

"He was like us." His words were thunder in the sky.

Ulf's nostrils flared in anger. He'd found many enemies worth killing over his many centuries; some shared a closer bond than others. "What did he call himself?"

"He named himself Kveldulf. I will never forget it."

"The Night Wolf."

Arnulf was silent, the words from Ulf's mouth cutting him.

"I have known others who used this name. You would do best to avoid him and his kin."

"Avoid him? He is the only thing I seek."

Ulf's eyes judged the warrior's intent and commitment and sighed. "It is not my place to stand in your way but know that you take us on a journey rife with danger."

"The danger brings me joy. The thought of his death is as beautiful as a freshly fallen snow to me." Arnulf stuck out his hand, and Ulf locked his hand around his forearm. "What is your name, Norseman?"

"Ulf Bodvarsson."

"Ulf Bodvarsson, you have tempered my flame of violence this day. I have never called a Norseman companion but that has changed," Arnulf said.

He tightened his grip on Ulf's arm, and Ulf smiled at him before squeezing the man's arm hard enough to bend an iron helm. "Companions."

"You owe me a new bow," Arnulf said, releasing him.

"I will find another for you. Tell me, where did you forge the arrowheads?"

"They were my father's. He saved them for when they came. Then when he came," his lip lifted, "I couldn't even draw my father's bow."

"Not all are ready when they are called to battle. The youth especially so."

"It will not happen a second time."

"Sons should be wiser than their fathers." Ulf was quiet for a moment reliving a distant memory. "Fathers should learn from their sons."

"With every day, the flame of vengeance grows brighter in my chest."

"The gods will see to it that justice is given. They know your plight. They see your struggle." Ulf nodded outward toward the field of battle. "They were witness to much this day and met many noble warriors."

"Witnesses to the destruction of their followers. God smiles upon us."

Ulf gave him a hard glance. "I lost many battle-brothers this day." *Is this man worth their lives?*

Arnulf blinked back his comment. No words escaping his throat. Both men contemplated the day's events, a smoldering violence smoking between them. Arnulf removed his linden-wood shield from his back. It was painted half blue, half white. "Bear this shield. It marks you as one of Ealdorman Leofwine's men." He glared intently at Ulf.

"Hide your arm rings away. If anyone asks, you stole them."

Ulf took the shield and removed his arm rings, stashing them in a small pouch on his belt. "Wise advice. I will seek my armor on the bridge."

"Leave the cuirass. You stood out in that relic."

"It was a gift from a past life."

Arnulf nodded to him as if he had agreed. "Then our battle is done this day. Let us rejoin Godwinson's army." He studied Ulf for a moment. "You will not anger of English boasts of prowess? I cannot protect you if you seek revenge among them."

Ulf lifted his chin. "My wrath is left for a select few. Not the men who survived this contest."

"Were you alone? Did your battle-brothers fall here?"

"Hardrada was my battle-brother," he said as he limped toward the forest edge. "My crew fell here this day. Men I had known since they were boys. I do not shed tears for them. They all went the warrior's way, sword and axe in hand. Honorable deaths. I will see them all again in Odin's Hall." He looked at Arnulf. "The Norns are fickle maidens. When you think you know their purpose, another presents itself."

"Pagans," Arnulf said with a shake of his head. "Your beliefs are an ancient blemish. With Godwinson at the helm, England will grow strong again."

"I will not pretend to know England's fate."

"We rest now, but soon we will take up our quest for Kveldulf."

"Your quest will be my own."

"Then let us start with a cup of ale," Arnulf said with a smile.

"Ale, ha. Mead is better. Odin favors it."

"Then you haven't had enough ale."

"Ale is for children, Arnulf, men drink mead."

Arnulf gave a long laugh that died on his lips as the two emerged from the woods onto the corpse-laden field. Crows bounced between the dead, others floated lazily in the sky like black smoke, and the two men walked silently among them.

THE END

A Word From Logan

Thank you for reading *Bridge of Kings*. The saga continues with the gritty, action-packed historical fantasy series The Oaths of Blood Saga. Start the rest of the series today! Click here to purchase.

The first novel of the saga, *Oaths of Blood*, is set during the First Crusade. A Norman mercenary and his mysterious allies are drawn into a centuries-long shadow war with an immortal order of knights bent on his destruction and the search for a relic known as the Black Chalice.

The second novel, *Sands of Bone*, follows the disastrous battle of Hattin, where a mysterious mercenary aids Balian de Ibelin in his attempt to defend Jerusalem from Saladin's victorious army. However, a new faction in the shadow war wants them both dead.

In the third novel, *City of Wolves*, the Order's quest for the Black Chalice brings a new crusade to Constantinople's doorstep. The motto of the Varangian Wolf Guard is Uphold the Oath. Will they do so to the last man?

If somehow you ended up here without joining the Irons Brigade - signing up for my newsletter - then let me extend an offer to subscribe to my mailing list. I send a newsletter once a month with writing updates, new releases, and deals. It's the best way to stay up to date and in the fight. Or if you prefer, please link with me on any of the social media platforms below.

> Instagram: @logandirons
> Website: logandirons.com

A quick note on the use of terms of Saxon and English. To one as old as Ulf, he certainly would have known the English as Saxons. The idea of England and being English is a long historical journey that deserves books upon books dedicated to its study. Short answer is that it was complicated. Historians consider the founding in 927 CE under Athelstan, a unification of Anglo-Saxon kingdoms and the solidification of England after the Battle of Battle of Brunanburh in 937 CE. Most people of the time probably didn't consider themselves English until much later. Large portions of northern lands under English control changed hands several times with various Scandinavian kingdoms until the fall of the Anglo-Saxon dynasty in 1066. But that is another tale.

I hope that we cross paths again. If not, I understand, and I leave you with this.

"The journey is long. The journey is hard. But it is your very own. And we do not go quietly into that great darkness without baring our fangs."

Uphold the Oath,

Logan D. Irons

About the Author

Logan is the author of the grimdark historical fantasy series The Oaths of Blood Saga.

A lifelong traveler, he has visited over 50 countries for both for work and for pleasure. Lifted in Arnold's childhood gym in Austria, asked his wife to marry him in an abandoned castle in Ireland, bartered for jewelry in a Kuwaiti souk, drank beers and sang German songs poorly at Oktoberfest in Munich, and burned a Viking ship during Hogmanay in Edinburgh.

Fantasy, historical fiction, and history novels dominate his library. In particular, the works of George R.R. Martin, Steven Pressfield, Bernard Cornwell, and Robert Jordan inspire his work. He currently resides in Virginia, a place with enough history to keep him busy until the end of time, with his wife, son, and a dog named Ronin the Barbarian.

If he has free time, which is rare, he throws axes (usually at targets), is physically active, and loves taking his family on adventures.

And he's convinced his nieces he's a werewolf...

LOGAN D. IRONS

www.logandirons.com

Printed in Great Britain
by Amazon